STO ✓

The CHICKEN in the TUNNEL

The CHICKEN in the TUNNEL

by Jane Thayer

Catherine, Woolley PSEUD.

illustrated by
TONY PALAZZO

WILLIAM MORROW and COMPANY
New York   1956

To Kathleen,
who met Squawky in the tunnel.

Squawky was a chicken. He was quite
little. He was scrawny and his feathers were
still scraggly. He lived on a farm with his
brothers and sisters and cousins.

x

5

One morning Mr. Hay, the farmer, said, "I must take some chickens to market in New York. I will take these and these." He put the chickens into crates.

Squawky saw that his cousins were going to market in New York. He didn't know what market in New York was, but it sounded exciting. He rushed over to Farmer Hay. "I want to go to market in New York too!" he squawked.

"You can't go, Squawky," said Farmer Hay. "You are too little. You are too scrawny."

But Squawky was anxious to go to market in New York. The minute Farmer Hay's back was turned, he stuck his head between the slats of one of the crates. He was so scrawny his head went right through.

Squawky squeezed one wing between the slats. He squeezed the other wing between the slats. He squeezed the rest of himself between the slats. And then he saw **Mr. Hay** coming back, ready to leave for New York.

"I am going to market in New York!" said
Squawky.

The crates were loaded onto a truck.
Farmer Hay drove off to market in New York.

Down the shady country road they went.
Squawky looked out of his crate and thought

that going to market in New York was lovely.
Down the big highway they went. Squawky

looked out of his crate, and the cars and
trucks whizzing by made him dizzy. I don't
like this much, he thought. He stuck his head
between the slats.

The closer they came to New York, the more cars and buses and trucks there were. Squawky hated them. He hated the noises and smells, too. He began to think, I don't want to go to market in New York. Finally he thought, I want to go home!
He squeezed one wing between the slats of the crate.

They came to the Lincoln Tunnel. The Lincoln Tunnel is a long tunnel under the Hudson River, with New Jersey on one side and New York on the other. Squawky's truck had to go through the tunnel.

Cars were going through the tunnel. Buses were buzzing through. Trucks were lumbering through. Cars, buses, trucks—all roaring and snorting and echoing, as they slowly moved through the long tunnel in two neverending lines.

The noises and smells and all the big trucks so close to him scared Squawky to death. I am going to get out of here and go home, he decided. He squeezed his other wing between the slats of the crate.

Traffic in the tunnel stopped for a minute. Squawky's truck had to stop. Suddenly

Squawky said, "Here I go!" He squeezed the rest of himself between the slats, flapped his wings, and landed on the road. He gave a loud squawk and headed for home.

Farmer Hay was facing the other way and did not see him. The policemen in the tun-

nel were watching the cars and did not see him. The drivers were driving and did not see him.

Traffic began to move. Squawky zigzagged between the lines of cars. The moving cars and buses and trucks made him dizzier and

dizzier. He almost ran into a tire. He nearly
ran under a car.

He flapped into the air as a wheel
almost ran over him.

A little girl was kneeling on the back seat of one of the cars. She looked out and saw Squawky. "There's a chicken running!" she cried.

"A chicken in the tunnel? Nonsense!" said her father.

"But I saw a chicken running!" the little girl said.

So her father stopped by the next policeman and shouted, "My little girl saw a chicken running in the tunnel."

"A chicken in the tunnel? Nonsense!" said the policeman.

"But she saw a chicken running!" the little girl's father said. "Do something before he gets killed."

So the policeman went to a telephone in the wall of the tunnel. He phoned the policeman at the entrance of the tunnel. He said, "A little girl saw a chicken running in the tunnel."

"A chicken in the tunnel? Nonsense!" said the other policeman.

"But she saw a chicken running!" the first policeman said. "Catch him before he gets killed."

So the policeman at the entrance of the tunnel phoned all the policemen in the tunnel. "A chicken is running in the tunnel. Catch him when he goes by." He hung up before they could say, "Nonsense!"

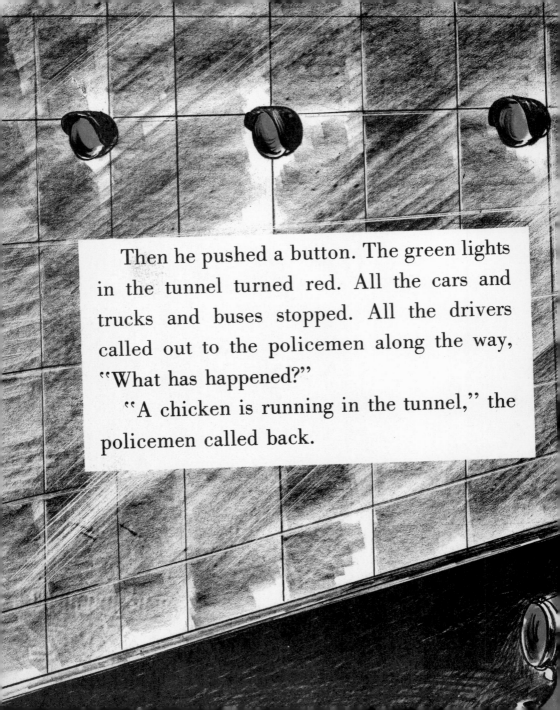

Then he pushed a button. The green lights in the tunnel turned red. All the cars and trucks and buses stopped. All the drivers called out to the policemen along the way, "What has happened?"

"A chicken is running in the tunnel," the policemen called back.

"For goodness' sake!" said the drivers. They craned their necks, looking for Squawky.

And suddenly here came Squawky, running between the cars, flapping his wings, squawking, and heading for home as fast as he could go!

A boy leaned out of a car window. "Come on, Squawky!" he cried. A lady said, "Keep going, Squawky!" A man called, "Attaboy, Squawky!"

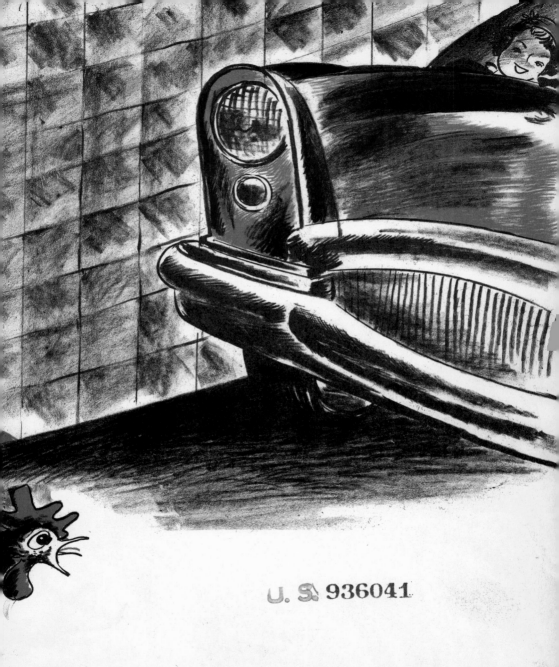

U. S. 936041

The lights stayed red. The cars and trucks and buses stood still. All the people cheered Squawky as he ran for home.

Squawky didn't answer. He just kept going.
At last, all out of breath, he reached the end

of the tunnel. Eight policemen were waiting
for him, and one of them caught Squawky.

"Three cheers for Squawky!" the people in the cars cried.

Then the policeman at the entrance of the tunnel pressed a button. The lights turned green. The cars and trucks and buses roared and began to move.

"Now what do we do with this chicken?" one policeman said.

"That truck will be coming back tonight," another policeman said. "We'll watch for it." They put Squawky in a box.

That night Farmer Hay's truck came rumbling back, full of empty crates. The policeman blew his whistle as the truck came out of the tunnel.

"You lost a chicken in the tunnel," the policeman said.

"Nonsense," said Farmer Hay.

"And here he is," the policeman said.

"Here I am!" said Squawky, popping out of the box.

"For goodness' sake!" said Farmer Hay. "How did you get here?" He put Squawky back in a crate.

Down the big highway the truck rumbled, farther and farther away from the terrible tunnel. It turned into the peaceful country road. At last the truck stopped. Squawky could tell by the cool country air, the quiet black night, and the sleepy sounds of the chickens on their roosts that he was safely home!

"Next time you'd better know where you're
going before you start!" Farmer Hay said to
Squawky, as he gave him his supper.

Squawky didn't say a word. He knew one place he *didn't* want to go to. He never again wanted to go to market in New York. He just hopped on his roost, and went to sleep.